Our Corner Store

Our Corner Store

Robert Heidbreder

Illustrations by Chelsea O'Byrne

Groundwood Books
House of Anansi Press
Toronto Berkeley

Groundwood Books / House of Anansi Press
groundwoodbooks.com

We gratefully acknowledge for their financial support of our publishing program
the Canada Council for the Arts, the Ontario Arts Council and
the Government of Canada.

Library and Archives Canada Cataloguing in Publication
Title: Our corner store / Robert Heidbreder ; illustrations by Chelsea O'Byrne.
Names: Heidbreder, Robert, author. | O'Byrne, Chelsea, illustrator.
Identifiers: Canadiana (print) 20190156554 | Canadiana (ebook) 20190156562 |
ISBN 9781773062167 (hardcover) | ISBN 9781773062174 (EPUB) |
ISBN 9781773062181 (Kindle)
Classification: LCC PS8565.E42 O97 2020 | DDC jC813/.54—dc23

The illustrations were done in gouache and colored pencils.
Design by Michael Solomon
Printed and bound in Malaysia

MIX
Paper from
responsible sources
FSC
www.fsc.org
FSC® C012700

To Carol Dale and Louise Hager,
community-minded small businesswomen,
book lovers and dear friends. RH

For Natasha. CO

Table of Contents

Ready, Set, Go!

Twenty hop-leaps,
            maybe more.

      Race you to . . .

            our corner grocery store!

Bert

We whirl in
      (our list lost on the way —
      OOOPS! —
            in our hop-about play)
but it's okay.
      Bert'll know.
            Bert always knows.
"Bert! Bert!" we shout.
      No Bert!
            We scout about,
            down aisles, round corners.
            No Bert!
So we crouch-sneak
      behind the meat counter
      where we're not ever to go.
            EVER!!!
            "That big freezer can slam-wham shut
            and then you're just kid popsicles!"
            (Bert told us.
                  So we know,
                        we know.)

      But where's Bert?
      "BERT?"
Then . . .
      out of the big walk-in freezer

springs Bert,
his long apron fluttering
like a huge, crazy, scary bird.
We scream.
He chases us
out of the store,
flapping, laughing wildly.
We crackle-rackle
through the fall leaves,
down the sidewalk,
back up our front stairs
and fly into the kitchen.
Mom stares at us, asks,
"Where are the groceries?
The list? Hmmm?"
"OOOPS!" we giggle
and whirl back to the store,
and Bert, once more.

The Cookie Jars

On the counter of the store
      stand glass cookie jars,
      gleaming high, filled tall to the top.
      They shine with taste.
           The cookies our mother makes
           are small, tight, one-bite types,
           but these are big, wide—
           cookie pancakes.
We always stare in hungry wanting.
      We think their yums
      would fill our tums.
      But they cost too much,
           way too much for us.
           For cookies such
           as those pancakes,
           we'd have to save for weeks.
                      Weeks, we think.
So they stay in their jars
      while we wish and dream,
      dream and wish.
We're wishing on cookie stars.

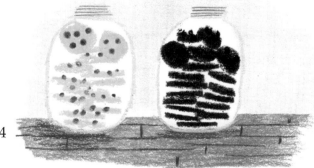

Tobias

Toby Cat lives in the storeroom mostly,
    with stacked packages,
    bundles of bags,
    tons of tins.
    Bert and Mr. Stanstones, the store owner,
        let us go in.
        We cuddle, cat-chat,
        knuckle-rub his head and chin,
        give him small scraps to nibble.
        His purring motor runs full throttle.
Sometimes we spot him
        in the alleys
        round about,
        rambling, scouting out,
        or low in hunting crouch.
Then we don't disturb him,
        or call him "Toby,"
        but silently mouth his full proper name:
            "Tobias C. Cat."
            "Tobias C. Cat."
We know he likes that:
        that we let him be . . .
                just CAT.

Mr. Stanstones

Mr. Stanstones owns the store.
    We like him,
        but we're kind of shy around him.
        He seems worried, sad.
        He stoops, shuffles,
        doesn't laugh or smile a lot.
At lunch, we ask our mom and dad about him.
    They say running a business is hard.
        There's a lot to worry about
        and money can be short.
We decide to give Mr. Stanstones a present.
    We draw pictures of the store:
        of Bert, of Toby, of Mr. Stanstones
        and Mrs. Stanstones,
        and lots of the cookie jars.
        All around the jars we put stars,
        like they're the shine of the store.
We roll up our pictures,
    tie them tight
        with the butcher string Bert gives us.

Then off we bound down to the store,
    clutching the pictures.
        We tumble in,
        dropping them
        all over the place.

"Oops! Sorry!"
we mumble
as we stoop to pick them up.
A big smile breaks out all over
Mr. Stanstones' face
as he unrolls them.
He even laughs.
Then he walks to the shiny cookie jars,
the store's stars,
and offers us each a cookie.
We stand stunned in cookie light
and carefully choose.
"Thank you! Thank you!"
we keep repeating,
rushing from the store,
FAST!
In case he changes his mind,
just in case!
We shuffle home slowly,
cradling the cookies
like they're golden glass
or precious stardust.
For days, days, we stow them away,
days, days.

We want our cookie magic to last.

Charge It

"Charge it! Charge it!"
　　　　We love those words,
　　　　　　think they're some
　　　　　　of the funniest we've ever heard.
We don't need money,
　　　　　　only the funny words
　　　　　　to fill the lists we carry.
Sometimes we don't use
　　　　　　the words at all.
　　　　　　　　We paw-paw the floor
　　　　　　　　and charge bull-like
　　　　　　　　all around the store.
Mrs. Stanstones, or Bert,
　　　　　　marks down what we buy,
　　　　　　　　gives us "the damages,"
　　　　　　　　as they say,
　　　　　　　　and we charge out
　　　　　　　　　　with a rumbling
　　　　　　　　　　　snort-shout.
　　(We sometimes forget
　　　　　　to take the groceries
　　　　　　and have to hurtle back.)
If we try to sneak onto the list
　　　　　　potato chips, pop, candy,
　　　　　　whatever we find tasty-dandy,

Bert lifts them away
and shouts out,
"Uncharge it! Uncharge it!"
We charge back home,
laughing,
until we yell, "Uncharge it!"
Then we freeze,
crumble-tumble down
and sprawl deep-asleep
on the ground.

The Big Freezer

"Please, Bert!" we plead.
    "PLEASE!!
    Let us see the big freezer!"
Bert glances round the store,
    puts his finger to his lips:
            "SHHHHHH!"
        And we all tip-toe,
        hunch-scrunched,
        into the cold dark,
        like spies or thieves.
It's midnight winter here,
    bright fall no more,
    behind the heavy shut door.
Bert switches on a dim light.
    Bit by bit we see meat
    hanging from hooks —
    sausages dangling
    with the look
    of fat party streamers,
    chicken, turkeys, beef sides, pork —
    all skin, bones,
    red, pink, fleshy-white tones.
Suddenly we're spooked.
    It's a skeleton house in here,
        Hallowe'en, spooky-scary-haunted.

Bert knows.
     So he lets us leave,
     but not before showing us
          the small handle, the latch
          that opens the door to freedom.
          "In case," he says. "Just in case!"
We escape and hurry home
               on the double.
          We decide not to tell Mom and Dad,
               not yet, anyway, not yet.
               We sure don't want Bert
               in any trouble.
Dad's going to make hamburgers
          for dinner, he says.
               But we see the freezer,
               still fixed cold-fast in our brains,
               and ask for pancakes.
               "Pancakes, please! Mom! Dad!
               Potato pancakes! PLEASE!"

Mrs. Stanstones

"Sometimes Tuesdays.
     Wednesdays? Could be.
     Saturdays. Hmm? . . . Maybe.
     But never, never on a Monday."
That's what Mrs. Stanstones says
     when we ask what days
     she works.
We like how she teases us,
     and we like even more
     the days she works at the store.
She tells us crow jokes:
     "What is a crow's favorite song?"
         "Crow, crow, crow your boat!"
         we chant in glee.
     "What is a crow's favorite drink?"
         "Caw-fee!" we cackle crazily.
  She lets us dust, stack the cans,
         which fit together like puzzles
         with a quick click.
  We pile carrots
     and potatoes
         into heaping mountain rows.
         The celery sticks
         we stick in like green streams
         flowing between the others.

We set the oranges
high up — a land of lots of suns.
But best of all,
we get to shine the glass:
Bert's butcher counter,
the cold ice-cream case,
the front hold-all display
and the cookie jars!
Shining, shining like the sun,
round and round
till shining's done.
Then she hugs us,
slips us some small change
and we charge home,
rich as bankers,
to clink all the change
into our own small,
smiling piggy banks.

Our Piggy Banks

"One for spendin', one for savin'.
That's what you are havin',"
        Mom and Dad explained
                as they handed us piggy banks,
                two big piggies each.
The *spendin'* one has a stopper
                stuck in its tummy.
                        When you unplug it,
                        the coins somersault out
                        in cheerful jingle-jangle.
The *savin'* one is solid,
                a plug-less pig.
                        To get all the money out,
                        you have to break the bank.
                        But we fast-learn if you tilt, tip,
                        shake, rattle and down-dip
                        just right, one coin will slip
                        out of the skinny top slot.
The big coins we clunk in *savin'*,
                the smaller bits we clink-clank
                into *spendin'*.

Sometimes we count the coins
                in the *spendin'* piggy
                up to where our coins stop.

Then one by one we drop
them back in,
counting the clink-clanks again.
We want to keep them safe.
So we hide them
under our beds
where little dust bunnies live.
(That's what Mother said.)
We're happy to think
that the big piggies
and the little bunnies
will be secret friends.

Pop Bottles

One, two, three, four, five, six, seven,
       all pop bottles go to Heaven!
After school on sunny-sure days,
       we jingle-jangle our old silvery wagon
              (Dad painted it shiny silver
              to hide the rust)
              down lanes, streets,
              round about bushy corners,
              searching for pop bottles
              to turn in for piggy-bank food.
When we get a shake-rattle-and-roll bunch,
       we clatter them into the store.
              Mr. Stanstones counts them out
              in seven-heaven rhyme chime,
              then hands us coins,
              one by careful one, and says:
              "Money got here, spend here too,
              or you'll turn to monkey stew!"
We smile wide as a mile,
              call out, "Thanks!"
              then hurry home
              to feed our hungry piggy banks.

Saturdays

"It's almost six!
　　　　We gotta go!"
　　　　Every Saturday we jump up
　　　　　　from the table
　　　　　　(the only day we're allowed)
　　　　　　and as fast as we're able,
　　　　　　speed down to Stanstones'
　　　　　　to help close up the store.
When we get there,
　　　　Bert lets us drop the blinds down
　　　　　　over the wide windows —
　　　　　　whoosh, whoosh!
　　　　　　We turn off the big fans
　　　　　　that whirl round-round,
　　　　　　in sleepy, snorey sound —
　　　　　　zooh, zooh!

Then shut off the humming lights —
bzzz, bzzz!
And carry Toby to Bert's car —
purr, purr!
Then Mr. Stanstones or Bert takes
the biggest, heaviest key
we've ever seen
and locks the wide door:
clunk-chunk-plunk-clang!
We all say goodbye.
Mrs. Stanstones gives the store (and us)
a pat
so it can sleep its quiet sleep
until Monday morning
comes peeking back round.

Jake

Jake's new to town.
>He just appears one day
>>and we all start to play
>>off and on,
>>at our house, at his, at school,
>>around-about the neighborhood.

He's riskier, bolder than we are.
>He has a jackknife, matches,
>>paper money stuffed in his pockets,
>>a big slingshot.
>>Sometimes he carries his BB gun
>>with him.
>>He's always offering us candies.

One day, we all dart into Stanstones'
>and start bugging Bert.
>Jake disappears
>>down the packaged-candy aisle.

We hear rustling.
>We see Jake stuff
>>some candies in his pocket,
>>knocking other candy off
>>with a crinkly-crackly racket.

"PUT IT BACK!" we shout
>without thinking.
>We just blurt it out.

Jake drops the candy,
        shoots from the store,
        down the block, to scoot home
        or somewhere private.
We don't say anything more
        to Bert or Mr. Stanstones
        but head down the aisle
        to put the candy back where it belongs.
After that,
        Jake mostly avoids us.
        Then one day,
        he just disappears from town.
We're sorry,
        sorry that Jake is gone so soon,
        sorry that we won't see him again,
        sorry that he couldn't stay our friend.

        We liked him.

Trick-and-Treat

Very scary costumes on,
    we go to trick-or-treat our first stop,
        Stanstones', where we usually get
        big, sticky candied apples
        and a bottle of their best pop.
Just as we hit the corner,
    Bert, Mr. Stanstones, Mrs. Stanstones
        all scream out of the store
        with a string of *EEEKKKS*
        in a fluttering line,
            streaming down the sidewalk.
            The store looks empty.
            Other customers follow.
            So we follow too, screaming,
            with our best Hallowe'en
            screeching.
Suddenly we all halt,
    peer round to hear
        a piercing *howl-growl-grrr*!
Out of the store
        strolls Toby, tail held high,
        a small, struggling mouse in mouth.
        He drops the mouse,
            who scutters off scared.

Toby pauses, soft-winks,
            U-turns and soft-paws
            straight back to his store home.
We stare,
        then clap at Toby's *trick* **and** *treat*.
                "Neat feat," Bert says.
                "Neat Halloween-cat feat!"

The Snow Storm

It starts Friday night.
     By Saturday morning
          the streets, sidewalks, houses
          shine high-quiet-winter-white.
Mother asks us to "plow down"
     to Stanstones' to get some milk.
          We bundle up,
          grab our small shovels,
          growl with plow noises
          and scoop out a skinny path
          to the door of the store.
It's shut tight, no lights on at all.
     So we scoop-shovel round about,
          mitten-wipe the windows free of snow.
Next, we start building:
     snow animals, snow girls, snow boys,
          funny misshapen snow toys
          all around the store,
       up and down the sidewalk.

More and more we build
        till the whole sidewalk
        is chock-a-block with
        crazy snow creatures of every sort,
        quietly waiting for the store to open.
Mr. Stanstones, Mrs. Stanstones,
        Bert, Mom and Dad,
        a bit worried,
        all arrive at the same time.
            They stare at the jumbled line,
            the wild piles of snow.
            They laugh loudly and clap.
"Looks like it's going
        to be a busy day,"
        Mrs. Stanstones says
        as she hands Mother the milk
        and sneaks us some small change.
        More loose loot
            to fatten up our piggy banks.

Lost

Bert phones:
>"Toby's gone,
>missing for two days now,
>ever since the big snowstorm."

We suit up and crunch out to search
>where he hunts, sleeps
>and hides from harm.

We keep our eyes peeled
>>for cat tracks, for fur,
>>for any signs of cat fight or hurt.

Often we play detective
>with magnifying glasses,
>>flashlights, all ears alert.
>>But this time it's for real.

Eyeballing everywhere,
>we turn up nothing,
>>NOTHING at all.

We crane necks up, up
and both shout,
"The warehouse ROOF!"
We know its ins and outs
since we sometimes play there,
though we're not supposed to.
It's Bert's Big Freezer cold.

We've never climbed the roof in the snow,
so we plan a new route
around,
         up,
               down,
                       over and through.
The snow makes it quiet
(the workers won't hear!)
but slippery-slick.

At the top,
            we head straight for the chimney —
            strong red brick, thick,
            a perfect chute for Santa.
We circle it . . .
            and there he is . . .
            TOBY!!
                  Curled up round
                  as a ball of yarn—
                  a surprise Santa present, early.
He meows, purrs
     and starts gently
     grooming his fur.
We gather him up
     and gingerly carry him,
     safe and sound,
     back through,
                  over,
                        down,
                              up and around.

When we bring him to
  Bert and Mr. Stanstones,
    he leaps from our arms
    and zip-zooms into his box
    in the storeroom,
    purring up his own winter storm.
We smile sky-wide
and people-purr along.

The Candy Jars

Around Christmastime every year,
   new jars suddenly appear
   next to the cookies,
      rainbowed with candies:
red-and-white swirly pinwheels,
green-and-white striped small
      puffy pillows,
      twirly-curly ribbons,
      yummy-gummy drops —
      little, big, brilliant colors all —
      and candy canes
      with twisty-turny stripes
         stretching
      round and round, up, around,
         beyond.

They shout out to us,
   "Buy me! Try me!
     I'm Christmas delicious."
We hurry home
  and give our piggy banks
   a good shake-rattle,
   pull the plug, and out the coins clatter.
Back to the store
  to buy as much candy as we can
   (or as much as Mrs. Stanstones
   will let us buy,
   with her quick eagle eye!).
Then back home,
  to eat some,
   to save some
   and to wait forever
   for Christmas to come.

The Grand Opening

We all pile into the car
> for the spring **"GRAND OPENING"**
> of a brand-new "Super Market!"
> > We somehow think
> > it will look like a big piano,
> > high up on legs
> > with top propped open,
> > > since we've only heard
> > > *grand* with *piano*.
> > > Maybe Superman will
> > > be there.

But it's big, flat, sits alone
> with squads of cars all around.
> There are no sidewalks near
> to run up and down,
> and no Superman.

Inside is brighter
> than high summer.
> Funny music hums
> like mosquitoes stuck in our ears
> or squirrels fiss-fussing on wires.

Food, noises, people surround us.

Carts click-clack up, down.
There's not a cat in sight.
We wander off, staring,
looking, eyeballing up,
around-about.

Soon we're lost
in a long aisle of boxes.
We panic,
hurry to find our parents.
A BIG VOICE yells at us,
"Stop running, kids! STOP! **NOW!**"
This startles us so that we smash
into a castle of cans.
They tumble down with a racket.
CRISH-CRUSH-CRASH!
We keep running, rushing
as the BIG VOICE chases us.
We swerve round a corner
and veer smack into our parents.
The BIG VOICE tells what we did,
as our mom and dad nod and say,
"Sorry!"
then usher us to help rebuild
the tower.
We all leave,
without buying anything
at the "**GRAND OPENING.**"

Teasing and Tricking

"Is your freezer running?"
        we ask Bert.
            "Yes," he answers.
            "Better go catch it," we shout.
            Then we dart out.
We put red watercolor spots
        all over us,
            whine through the back door
            of the store,
            sobbing, "Sick, sick, we're sick!"
When Mrs. Stanstones says,
        "My! Oh! My!"
            we rub them off
            with a damp cloth,
            and out we fly.

We drop off a long list
      and say, "It's important.
           It's for mother's party.
           We'll be back for pick-up.
           Soon. Real soon."
The list is crammed with candy,
      potato chips, pop
      and alphabet soup,
        scrawled in our big, loopy printing.
Then we don't go back.
      They'll know it's a joke.
"You're little cards,
      wild cards," they laugh.
        "But just you wait!
        We have a plan, a plan,
        you little cards!"
        "Baseball cards," we laugh.
        "We're star players! Aces!"
        we say as we go bat-swinging
        out the swinging door
        and home-run home.

Hurting Bert

"Baldie Bert,
    head like a ball.
    Take a rag
    and shine it all . . . "
We skip to the store,
    chanting out
    our made-up rhyme,
        giggling, clapping,
        grinning all the time.
Bursting into the store
    through the back door,
        we blurt it out to Bert.
        (He's helping Mrs. Gretzinger.)
        They both looked startled.
He turns away from us.
We know we've made a mistake,
        that we've hurt Bert.
            We slink home,
        where we tell Mom and Dad
        how bad we feel —
            before that Mrs. Gretzinger can.
            (We know what *she* thinks of
            children.)
They say,
            "Well, you know how to fix it,
            don't you?"

At the kitchen table
        we write sorry letters,
        best as we're able.
        We don't ask for help.
        They should be from us,
                just us, we decide.
Then we draw Bert
        surrounded by stars,
        yellow-gold stars, big as cars.
                (Bert knows we love drawing stars.
                We love cars too.)
We shake some change
        from our piggy banks,
                the special big-money ones,
                and slowly shuffle back,
                dragging our heavy feet,
                still feeling nasty-mean.
But Bert understands right away.
        He takes the pictures,
                tapes them up behind
                his butcher-block work counter.
        But he hands us back the money.
"I know, I know," he says.
        "I was a kid once too,
                believe it or not!
                I had hair then, lots of it,
                as much as you two put together."

He wildly polishes his head
    with an old rag,
        tousles our hair,
        and with a warm laugh
        slices us each a thin piece of
        summer sausage,
        our best meat treat ever.
We feel free again, light,
    so glad that Bert
        lets us leave our meanness behind.

The Great Robbery

"Picnic time,"
  Mom and Dad call up to our room.
    "Spring picnic time real soon.
    Better get your money
    in case the concession stand's open."
Grabbing our piggy banks,
    we jangle some money,
    a little, then more,
    more, from the wiggling piggies.
We hurl downstairs
    and leave the banks
      lying about on our beds,
      tired, piggy sleepy-heads.

When we get back home,
    the door's wide open.
      "Thieves!"
      Dad whispers.
      "Robbers!"
      We get the shivers.
Silently, we all search the house,
    room by room.
      Mother carries a broom—
      only she knows why.
      ("Gonna try to fly?
      Fly away, Mom?" we quietly tease.)

When we get to our room,
our piggy banks are gone.
                    We freeze.
        Mother drops the broom.
                    We all jump up.
"Run down to Stanstones'.
        See if they saw anybody,
            anyone, anything, anywhere,"
        she whispers.

"Bert! Bert!" we cry.
        "We've been robbed."
        Bert smiles broadly.
        "Tricksters!
                    Little wild cards!"
"No! NO!" we cry. "It's true.
        We tell you. It's true."
Bert just laughs harder.
        "Bert, it's not funny! It's TRUE!"
            "Okey-dokey." He grins. "I believe you.
        Now come on over, my rovers,
        and let me slice you up a piece
        of your best sausage treat.
        Come on! Choose your treat!"
    We don't really want to,
    but we peer into the big glass case anyway.
        We stare, and stare again.

There by the bacon,
ham and pork chops
sit our piggy banks.
Our mouths fall open.
Our eyes pop wide.
Then we squirm
with delight and surprise,
just as Mom and Dad come
into the store.
Hooting, hollering,
the grownups—
Bert, Mom, Dad, Mrs. Stanstones,
even sad Mr. Stanstones, all yell:
"Gotcha! Gotcha good,
as we knew we sure could.
Tricky little cards like you
oughta learn to be careful.
Yes, they should!"
We laugh too, but not a lot . . . and after a bit.
We like that the joke is on us, mostly,
that they all tricked us back.
But we like even more
that our piggy banks
are safe and sound,
not broken, smashed
or spilled.

We leave the store happy all around,
   but planning in our heads
   a good trick, a really good one,
   a fun one, right back on them.
   They'd better watch out!

Comic Books

Stanstones' sells comic books:
    stacks and stacks, it seems,
        rows and rows
        on creaky spin-about racks.
We eye them
    as round and round
        they slowly go.
        But we don't buy many.
        They cost too much money.
    But it's okay,
    since many days
    Mrs. Stanstones lets us choose one,
        squat behind the front counter,
        turn the picture pages
        and work to read the hard words.
        Toby nudges in and purrs.
If Mrs. Stanstones is free,
        she'll grab a stool or chair
        and read along with us,
        making the hard words easier.
We giggle as we read,
        then we get to borrow one
        to share with Dad and Mom,
        who always say,
        "Hey, what star readers you are,

our little baseball cards.
Who taught you? Hmmm?"
We don't tell them
how Mrs. Stanstones helps us,
but we're sure they guess.
We grin, nod our heads and say,
"You know,
Toby's a good reader too!"

Closing

Home from our farm-summer holiday,
  we bounce down to Stanstones'
    straight away,
    itching to see Bert, Toby,
    Mr. Stanstones and Mrs. Stanstones,
    and to tell them about
    our new summertime kitten.
The store looks different — quieter, emptier.
      Toby is roaming around,
      padding up and down,
      meowing a kind of lost sound.
"Bert! Bert! What's happening? What?"
      "We're closing, shutting down!"
        "Why, Bert, why?" we cry.
Mrs. and Mr. Stanstones walk over slowly.
      "Money's short.
        We don't have enough . . .
        to keep going . . . to compete.
        Too many bigger superstores
        are opening now, too many.
We told your mom and dad,
        but they wanted to wait
        until you got back.
        They didn't want you to feel sad
        while you were away on holiday."

But we are sad.
   We don't know what to say.
   We look at them, at Toby,
     hold back hot tears
     and go out, away.
     But the sadness stays.
In the next few days,
   we go back to help pack,
   clean and tell customers
   the sad, bad news.
     We pat Toby,
     whisper his name
     over and over
     to keep him purring,
     loved, happy.
Finally the last day comes,
   the closing up, the shutting down.
   A lot of people stand around
   saying,
   "Thank you! Good luck!
   We'll miss you!"
Mrs. and Mr. Stanstones walk over
   and hand us a wrapped package.
     We open it right away.
     It's the huge,
     shiny cookie jars.
"New piggy banks, cookie-jar piggy banks,"
     they joke, as they jangle

some big shiny coins they've put in.
"To hold lots and lots of loot."
Bert brings Toby over,
        cuddled in his arms,
        for one final pat and hug.
        Toby meows.
        His sandpaper tongue licks us.
"Remember to visit Toby and me, remember!
        We're gonna miss you!" Bert says.

Then Bert shuts the door
            tight, secure, for sure
            for the last time.
            For the very last time,
            he locks the door
                    on our corner
                    grocery store.

Then

When my sister and I talk about growing up, we remember the freedom we had then.

We could explore, make mistakes, find friends, grow in our own way and live outside our small family. We were free to roam.

Bert, Mr. and Mrs. Stanstones, and Toby were a big part of this freedom. But it couldn't have happened without the trust of our parents.

As both Mom and Dad used to say:

> *You're wild cards, free to roam,*
> *with not just one, but many a home.*